AS DIFFERENT AS NIGHT AND DAY...

I don't know how my brother came to see everything so upside down from me. For him, night is day, sleep is awake. It's as though time is split between us, and we only pass by each other as the sun rises or sets. Usually, for me, that's enough.

MORNING GIRL

SCHOLASTIC INC.
New York Toronto London Auckland Sydney

Copyright © 1992 by Michael Dorris.
All rights reserved. Published by Scholastic Inc., 555 Broadway, New York, NY 10012, by arrangement with Hyperion Books for Children.
Printed in the U.S.A.
ISBN 0-590-67925-2

7 8 9 10   40   02 01 00 99

*Portions of this book, in altered form,
have appeared in* Scope *magazine.*

Grateful acknowledgment is made for permission
to reprint the following copyrighted material:
Excerpt from *The Diario of Christopher Columbus's
First Voyage to America, 1492–1493,*
Abstracted by Fray Bartolomé de las Casas,
Transcribed and translated by
Oliver Dunn and James E. Kelley, Jr.
Copyright © 1989 by Oliver Dunn and James E. Kelley, Jr.,
Published by the University of Oklahoma Press.

For the little girls who listen,
And the mother who tells wonderful stories

MORNING GIRL

The name my family calls me is Morning Girl because I wake up early, always with something on my mind. Mother says it's because I dream too hard, and that I don't relax even in sleep. Maybe she's right—in my dreams I'm always doing things: swimming or searching on the beach for unbroken shells or figuring out a good place to fish. I open my eyes as soon as the light calls through the smoke

1

hole in the roof, sift the ideas that have come to me in the night and decide which one to follow first.

I don't tell this to anyone because they might misunderstand, but I like the aloneness of the early morning. I try to step gently on the path so that the sounds I make will blend into the rustle of the world. Father taught me how to swim on land, careful as a turtle. You'll see more if you're quiet, he told me. Things don't hide or wait for you to pass. And, it's more polite.

Another thing: if the day starts before you do, you never catch up. You spend all your time running after what you should have already done, and no matter how much you hurry, you never finish the race in a tie. The day wins.

I tried once to explain all this to my little brother, but he just blinked at me, asked me who said it was a race in the first place? See, he likes the darkness best, especially when there are no clouds and no moon. Sometimes he shakes me until I look as he points out the patterns he sees in the sky, the tracks made of white sand. He's sure what we see is part of another island, even bigger than the one where we live or than the one that appears in a pond when the water is very smooth. He thinks we're like birds floating above that sky island, very, very high.

I don't know how my brother came to see everything so upside down from me. For him, night is day, sleep is awake. It's as though time is split between us, and we only pass by each other as the sun rises or sets. Usually, for me, that's enough.

Mother promises that someday my brother and I will be friends, like she and her brother Sharp Tooth finally got to be. She whispers when she tells stories of how my uncle acted when he was a boy— how twice he laughed at her when she got into trouble or how he told a lie and never untied it, ever, with the truth. She became very still, closed her eyes, and took a deep breath at that memory, but then she shook her head, looked into me the way only she can do, and said that she used to believe she'd never forget what he had done; but look, she has. And now Sharp Tooth is exactly the brother she wants, the person in the whole world who remembers important things from when she was a young girl, who remembers Grandfather when he was alive and before he grew old.

I don't answer what I think: that *my* brother is

different from *hers*. Because my brother is her son, Mother doesn't know him as others do. As I do. When he's away from her sight, he eats too much. When she isn't there to hear him, he doesn't understand how to be quiet. And who knows what he does all night while the rest of us are asleep?

Just before dawn today I woke and found him sitting on the edge of my mat, watching me with big eyes.

"What's the matter?" I asked him. My voice was not soft. He wouldn't let me be alone even at night.

"Nothing," he said. "What do you mean? You're always complaining."

"I'm not the one who stares like a duck," I answered. "I'm not the one who can't stay asleep like a normal person."

"Ghosts," Father sighed from his hammock. "My house is filled with ghosts. They talk to each other all night. I'll have to build a new house. I'll live there in peace. It will be wonderful."

"Oh yes. I'll come with you." Mother's voice was unhappy as a fish pulled into the air from the sea. "Let's escape from such cruel ghosts who will not let people have their rest."

4

I could have explained that it was my brother's fault, but it would have done no good. Father would only have made more jokes and Mother would have said, "We'll listen later, Morning Girl."

I stood up, squeezed the stiffness from the back of my neck, and gave my brother a parting frown that I hoped would leave him very worried. That did no good, either, for he was already back on his own mat, curled into a comfortable position, pretending to be dreaming. His eyes were closed tightly, and his mouth was smiling.

Outside, at least, belonged to me, since no one else was around. I could do anything, go anywhere. I could walk or run, I could climb or swim, I could watch the ocean or slip into the mango grove, keep very quiet until the birds forgot I was there and began to talk to one another again.

The day welcomed me, brushed my hair with its breeze, greeted me with its songs. I raised my arms high and stretched. I let the rich scent of the large red flowers color my thoughts, and the perfume gave me an idea of how to use my special time. I would search for the most beautiful blossoms and weave them together into necklaces for Father and

Mother. If I hurried I could finish before they rose for the second time, and they would find my gifts waiting at the entrance to our house.

As I was working, my mind rushed ahead to what I knew was sure to happen. Mother would come outside first, see the necklaces, and go back in to get Father. Then they would return to the doorway together, him rubbing his eyes and grumbling until he noticed what lay at his feet.

"Look at this," he would cry, as if he were completely surprised, and Mother would press her hands together and say, "How unusual! How well made!"

"Where could these amazing necklaces have come from?" Mother and Father would ask each other as they placed my flowers around their necks.

And they would still be wearing them, still be happy with me, when finally, late in the morning, long after everyone else, my brother woke up.

CHAPTER TWO

STAR BOY

You know how it is when you're on the beach on a white sunny morning and you shut your eyes tight? What you see isn't exactly dark, at least not dark the way it's dark when you're inside your house at night and you can't make anything out, when every noise is a question you can't answer. What you see with your eyes closed during the day is something different. It's like deep water, a pond that's draped with shade. I don't know what makes it happen—the fins of tiny fish, or their eyes, the sparkle of agates—but there are lights moving down there, something to watch. It's the same on a night when there's no moon and you look straight into the sky: the more you watch, the more you see. Grains of white sand, it looks like, and sometimes one drops so fast you can hardly follow it before it's lost.

What I don't like is nothing. I don't mean I like everything, because I don't. I don't like it when my sister wakes me up. I don't like to eat fish with too many bones. I don't like those hungry bugs so small you don't know they're there until they bite you. But mostly I don't like . . . nothing. You know: *nothing*. I don't like it when there's nothing to hear, nothing to taste, nothing to touch, especially when there's nothing to see. Those times, I don't know where I am. The first night I woke up and noticed that everyone was invisible, I held perfectly still and disappeared. I became nothing, too, and I didn't know how to get back. Finally I talked to myself, whispered a little song my father sings when he speaks to the birds, excusing himself for bothering them. I rubbed the tip of my thumb against the tip of my fingers. I touched my tongue to my lips and tasted salt from the ocean, and I waited that way until the day remembered us, and returned.

"Why are you awake so early?" my mother asked me that morning. "Are you becoming the same kind of flower as your sister, the kind that bends to the east and calls the sun?"

I didn't like being anything like my sister, who in fact is called Morning Girl because she gets up before everyone else, so I told a different story.

"I don't need sleep anymore," I said.

"That's too bad." My mother shook her head and smoothed my hair flat. "How will you dream if you don't sleep? How will you hear yourself?"

I thought about this problem.

"Maybe you're a bat," my mother suggested, smiling at me, "and will dream all day while the rest of us work. How lucky for you."

I thought of bats and how they race through the dark sky fast as late summer rain. I thought of how the wind would feel against my skin if I could fly.

"It's true," I said. "I *will* sleep today."

"And hang upside down from the limb of a tree?"

9

asked Morning Girl, who always listened to what anyone said even though it had nothing to do with her. "I want to see that. Maybe I'll poke you with a stick."

"And maybe during the night I'll land in your hair," I told her. "Maybe I'll build a nest."

"Bats don't make nests," she pointed out, but still she raised her hand to her head at the idea.

"Maybe I'm a new kind of bat."

"What is it about the night that you like?" my mother asked, to stop the argument—but not just for that reason. She was truly interested and always listened closely to what I said. Now she stopped cleaning a manioc root and looked at me.

"I like . . . ," I began, and thought back to the white sand scattered on the sky's black beach. "I like the stars. I like to look down at them."

"You don't look *down* at the sky," Morning Girl contradicted. "You look *up*."

"Maybe not if you're a bat," my father said, his voice very serious. His eyes were still closed, and so it seemed as though his words came from no-where. We couldn't tell if he was joking or not. "But no one is asking the right question," he continued. "Why *don't* bats sleep at night? Perhaps they like the same things as this Star Boy does."

Star Boy.

That was the first time I heard my new name. Star Boy. Before that I was called "Hungry" because that's what I was most of the time. I liked "Star Boy" much better. No one spoke as we all listened, tested the weight of the words.

Star Boy.

My mother smiled. "Who is talking?" she asked at last. "Who has found such a good question? Who has thought of such a fine name for my son?"

"It is the father of a bat," said my father. "The father of a morning flower. It is the husband of the mother of a bat and a flower. It is a man who is surrounded by people who talk when others are trying to sleep. I think I must be in the wrong family, since I am the only one who knows the value of rest. I think—"

My mother looked at Morning Girl and me with her eyebrows raised, then slipped a piece of clean fruit between my father's lips to stop his words. We all watched while he chewed. He still did not open his eyes.

"No," he said after he swallowed. "This is not the wrong family. There is only one person who knows where to find fruit so sweet, only one person with fingers so gentle."

My mother lowered her eyes, but she was pleased. "Why do bats like the dark?" she asked me, returning to our conversation. "Tell us, Star Boy."

When she used my new name I knew it was now mine for good, and at that moment I decided that I would become an expert, a person who would be asked questions about the night and who would know the answers.

"Because it's big," I said. "Because there are special things to see if you watch closely. Because in it you can be dreaming even if you're awake. Because someone must remember the day while others sleep and call it when it's time for the sun to come home."

My father opened his eyes at last, propped himself on his elbows, and nodded.

"Star Boy," he said.

M○RNING GIRL

When things around me are right, I forget to notice: I don't remember days that aren't too hot or too wet or nights when the breeze blows hard enough to move the bugs away, but not hard enough to beat the palm leaves against the trunks of the trees. When I'm eating fruit, it's just . . . fruit, unless it's too ripe and dribbles down my chin or so tough that my teeth get sore from biting into it.

If something isn't too much or too little, I don't pay attention. When Father repairs the holes in his fishnet after the evening meal, I watch without really seeing him. He's doing what he's *supposed* to do—his eyes alert for a ripped square, his fingers finding and tying, his voice to Mother too low except for her ears. Or, in midday when it's just Mother and me inside, her humming or telling me about when she was a girl my age while she pounds roots for dinner, the world fits together so tightly, the pieces like pebbles and shells sunk into the sand after the tide has gone out, before anyone has walked on the beach and left footprints.

In our house, though, my brother was the footprints. He messed up the niceness for me. Just being himself, he was too loud: making jokes when he should be serious, talking when he should listen, running when he should sit, banging two rocks together for no reason except to disturb the silence, interrupting Mother or Father to ask questions he already knew the answers to, once putting a tiny green lizard on my mat as I was trying to hear the first morning sounds.

It was as though Star Boy didn't truly belong in

our family, and when I was angry I imagined what it would be like if he weren't around, how perfect each minute could be. I closed my eyes, and I could see it: Father and Mother and me, never arguing or raising our voices—and usually, at that very instant, as if I had called his name, my brother would come stomping through the doorway, bringing dirt where I'd just swept, throwing his arms around Mother when she was trying to finish a story, or wanting Father to leave his work and go outside to look at some mouse hole or an oddly shaped cloud.

My brother never simply put his footprints in the sand, he *jumped* in it, *kicked* it, dug holes, pried rocks loose and threw them into the sea to see the splashes. But whenever I pointed out how he acted—and, the truth is, I did it only so that he would learn and not make the same mistakes a second time, only so that he would understand how good it could be if he didn't ruin everything—*I* was the one who got the raised eyebrows, as if he were my fault.

Yet Star Boy was a trouble I was used to, an ordinary trouble that, really, was not so bad. Not like a real trouble.

I remember very well the afternoon when Mother told me her news. She and I were sitting side by side, spinning strings of cotton. She was showing me how to twine the new strands together with the old, the hardest part.

"I'm sure you're very lonely," she said.

Mother was usually correct in what she thought about me, she understood me so well, so I considered her words before I answered.

"I don't think I'm lonely."

"Oh yes," she said. "You just don't realize it because you don't know how happy you will be with a new baby sister to play with."

"I don't have a new baby sister," I reminded her, but at that moment I began to wonder. I remembered how many whispers Mother and Father and Grandmother had been having lately, and then I realized that it had been a long time since Mother had gone off for her days in the women's house.

"What shall we name her?" Mother asked, watching my face. "She's not a real person until she has a name, not a human being, not your sister or my daughter. After she comes into the world we have to decide right away who she is. Father and I need you to help us. And Star Boy, too."

Star Boy. For a moment I had forgotten about him and was picturing a life with just Mother, Father, and the new sister.

"When is she coming?" I wanted to know.

"Not so soon." Mother smiled. "But I've begun to feel her approach. She reminds me of you because she's so strong."

I discovered that I liked this new sister already.

"Does Star Boy know?"

"I'm going to tell him tonight."

I liked this new *secret* sister very much, and even more later on, when I listened to Mother and Star Boy talking in front of the house.

"How do you know it's a sister?" he asked. "Why not a brother? Why not a wonderful parrot, like the one those strangers brought with them from another island last year?"

"It *could* be a brother," Mother said. "But I don't think so. I'm certain it will not be a wonderful parrot."

"If it's another sister I'll leave and go someplace else," Star Boy warned. "I'll find a house that has no sisters at all."

"Wait before you decide." Mother put her hand on Star Boy's head. "Every sister is different."

"Yes," I called from where I sat. "This new sister will never let you put a green lizard on her sleeping mat. This new sister will chase you to your new house and then make you stay there."

"Maybe we *should* wish for a wonderful parrot," Mother said softly, and went to tell Father.

A turn of the moon later, Mother was gone when I came home. Father said she went to visit Grandmother for a while. I could tell he was worried because he held his mouth in a thin line when he thought I wasn't watching. He worked in the house all day, putting the big mats outdoors to air in the sun and retying the palm fronds on the roof so that the rain would not drip through during the next storm. If Star Boy and I asked nicely, he played guessing games with us, but the one thing he wouldn't do was talk about the new sister. He said it was too soon.

"Shouldn't we try to think of names?" I suggested. "That's like a riddle."

"We'll know the right name when the time comes," Father said. "People choose their own name, or it chooses them. That was how it was with you, Morning Girl. How could we have known before we met you what you would be like?''

"If you *had* known . . . ," Star Boy began.

"How glad we would have been," Father finished for him. "But as for you, a bat who sleeps during the day . . ."

"An expert on the night," Star Boy insisted.

I didn't know how long Mother would be away, but the day passed slowly without her. I noticed, because too much was missing: Her voice, calling me to eat. Her fingers working on my hair when it was tangled or stuck out from my head after sleep. The quiet warm sound of her conversations with Father. Even Star Boy watched the path for her return, though he pretended not to.

But instead of Mother, it was Father who entered our house the next day at an hour when usually he would be fishing.

"Mother will come home tomorrow," he told Star Boy and me.

"With the new sister," I reminded him. "Have you seen her yet?"

19

Father sat down and rested his back against the wall. He looked tired, but not sleepy. He patted the ground for Star Boy and me to come near.

"There isn't a new sister this time," he said.

"It's a new brother!" Star Boy clapped his hands together.

"No. Not a new brother, either. Not this time." Father's voice was different in a way I couldn't recognize. It wasn't angry or joking or . . . fatherly. It was almost as though he was talking to himself and we were overhearing, as though he was leaving out something. His eyes were the color of a night sky when it's raining.

I looked at Star Boy and saw that he was afraid. His body was stiff, his knees against his chest, his hands balled into fists, his mouth shut, his shoulders pulled up like the wings of a bird waiting for a wind storm to end before it took off. He glanced at me, and it was so strange because I think that was the first time we ever actually saw each other. Of course, I knew what he looked like. Sometimes I could tell when he was behind me, without turning around. But I never let myself wonder much about him. He was just . . . I don't know . . . always there, the opposite of me, and now, suddenly, I realized that in some ways we were the same.

"Is Mother sick?" I asked Father, but I kept my eyes on Star Boy, and he stared back, waiting to see what I heard.

Father sat up, put one of his strong arms around each of us, and drew us close to him. "Your mother is well," he said, and I saw Star Boy relax, so I did, too.

"But, there's something." Star Boy watched Father very carefully.

"She is . . . ," Father sighed, and squeezed my shoulder. "She is disappointed."

"Because the new sister didn't come," I whispered.

Father didn't answer right away, but I knew: he was also disappointed.

And so, I realized, was I. Worse than disappointed. I felt the way I feel when some big girl, like my cousin Feet, is playing too rough in the sea, kicking water at me even when I tell her to stop. That makes me want to cry.

*   *   *

21

When Mother returned from Grandmother's house, she was very glad to see me. She hugged me against her for a long time, stroking my head and saying my name over and over. Finally she stepped back, taking hold of my hands. Her face was sad, yet I didn't know what to say to her. Then I heard a noise, and behind her, in the doorway, I saw my brother. He paused, as if listening for some signal, for some sign from me.

"Look, Mother," I said. "Star Boy's here. He has been waiting and waiting and waiting for you to come home."

She turned, and Star Boy ran into the house, wrapped his slim brown arms around her waist, and pressed his head to her stomach. I saw a tiny flame light in Mother's eyes, and when she knelt to touch Star Boy's face and to kiss his cheeks, my brother's shoulders lost their hunch, forgot their fear. I took a breath, and the tightness left my stomach. Seeing Mother and Star Boy like that was so right, so how it should be, that for a long moment I didn't wish it was me in her arms. I didn't notice a thing.

CHAPTER FOUR

STAR BOY

I won't go home. I've been hiding in these rocks all day. I didn't come out when I heard Morning Girl call my name, even though she walked very close to where I crouched. I made myself look like a rock and didn't move. I shut my eyes, stopped breathing. I thought about how the sun warmed my surface, making shadows around all the parts where I stuck out. I thought how good it would feel when the waves splashed high enough to sprinkle drops of water onto my skin. I hoped that some birds might land on my back, but then I remembered how sharp the claws on their feet could be, and I hoped that the birds would find another rock instead.

My sister passed by without noticing me because she was searching for a human boy who might want to eat his midday meal, not for a stone who didn't need food, who didn't need to sleep under a roof, who had no worries that he had made a mistake.

The afternoon went by, and I thought about everything a rock could think: wind, rain, the things that could crawl out of the night and run across my face. I was glad I didn't have to drink because then I'd be thirsty. I wondered if the other rocks all around me had made mistakes, too. In a very low voice, I asked them, but even though I listened well, listened as a rock listens and not as a boy listens, I heard no answer. Maybe they were afraid to speak. Maybe they were waiting to see what kind of a rock I turned out to be. Maybe they heard my mother's footsteps before I did.

I barely opened one eye, so narrowly that the

light flashed the way it does when the sun strikes against shallow water. It was strange to watch my mother when she didn't know I was there, so strange that I almost forgot my mother was my mother. To a rock, she was just a small woman who sat looking out to sea, whose hair blew away from her face with every breeze, whose fingers worked the dry grasses in her lap into a tight coil, who spoke her thoughts aloud because she had no idea anyone was listening.

"Where could Star Boy have gone?" she wondered to herself. "Everyone is so worried that he has sailed to another island or flown high into the air to join those stars who gave him his beautiful name."

She sighed, waited for a moment, then continued. She was close enough that I could have touched her if my arms had turned back into arms and I became human once again.

"But Star Boy would not leave without saying good-bye," my mother decided. "Even if he had made a mistake, even if he had played in his father's canoe and then forgotten to pull it high enough up the beach so that the tide would not carry it away, he would know that we would miss him too much if he disappeared."

I closed my eye and concentrated on being a rock. I sank so deep into the ground that no digging stick could roll me from my hole. I became so hard that no tree or bush could take root on my surface. I slowed my thoughts until the quietness of the earth wrapped me in its heavy cotton. Somewhere far, far away from where I was, I heard my mother stir, stand up. I didn't feel her hand, soft against my foot, as she searched for more grass to weave. I wondered if she would cry out in the night for me, as she did once for the new sister who had not arrived after all. If she did, I would come back, but not until.

After my mother left, I passed another long, long time by myself. There was nothing to think about except the cramps in my knees where they bent to fit beneath me. I licked my lips to see if any dew had formed, and I twitched so quickly, when a buzzing insect of some kind landed near my ear, that if people were watching they'd think their eyes were playing tricks. I became heavy, solid enough to anchor any boat no matter how strong the ocean pulled.

There are things I noticed as a rock that I never realized as a boy. I could feel the movement of a shadow on my body as the sun slid across the sky. There was a line that divided heat from cool, which very slowly crept up my leg, across my back, onto my cheek. I could smell the skin of my arm, warm and sweet and like nothing else in the world. I could count my teeth with the tip of my tongue, find the silent crickets that called to each other from each of my wrists. I got to know myself as a rock even better than I had known myself as a person, one part at a time, with no rushing and nothing to make me hurry past something important. By the hour that the sky turned red, I had learned a great deal that I would not forget.

That's when I heard my father coming. He stopped almost exactly where my mother had sat, and hunched down as he often does when he's thinking.

"How fortunate that my wife's brother, Sharp Tooth, found my canoe," my father said to himself. "How fortunate that there was no damage and that it is now once again safely pulled far up on the beach. How relieved my son, Star Boy, would be to know that all turned out so well, but how can I inform him?"

I changed from being a rock to being an ear, a huge ear that could hear every word.

"But even if the canoe had floated away, even if it had vanished beneath the waves, it is only a canoe," my father continued. "It can be replaced with a few days' work, especially if I have a strong son to help me hollow it out. But nothing can replace a son. Not even a new child that might someday come. Not even a good daughter who was lonely for her brother all day, who was afraid that he was hungry or thirsty or didn't know how to come home."

I tried to imagine Morning Girl worrying about me. It was difficult.

"When Morning Girl told me she had been careless with my canoe," my father said, "I was very annoyed."

"But it wasn't her!" I shouted.

My father leapt to his feet, looked in every direction. "Star Boy?" he called. "Star Boy?"

I unfolded myself, became my father's son again because I heard the pleasure in his voice. Already I could see my mother's face when I walked through the door to our house. And behind her, my sister's eyes are bright.

MORNING GIRL

The water is never still enough. Just when I can almost see my face, when my eyes and my nose and my mouth are about to settle into a picture I can remember, a fish rises for air or a leaf drops to the surface of the pond or Star Boy tosses a pebble into my reflection and I break into shining pieces. It makes no sense to him that I'm curious about what people see when they look at me.

"They see *you*," he said, as if that answered my question. We were searching for ripe fruit on the trees behind our house.

"But what *is* me?" I asked him. "I wouldn't recognize myself unless I was sitting on the bottom of a quiet pool, looking up at me looking down."

"You are . . . *you*." He lost his patience and walked away to find his friend Red Feathers.

But what did "you" mean? I knew my hands very well. I study them when I trim my nails with the rough edge of a broken shell, making them smooth and flat. I could spread my fingers and press them into wet sand to see the shape they leave. Once I tried to do that with my head, but all I got was a big shallow hole and dirty hair.

I knew the front of my body, the bottoms of my feet. I knew the color of my arms—tan as the inside of a yam after the air has dried it—and if I stretched my tongue I could see its pink tip.

"Tell me about my face," I asked Mother one day when we were walking along the beach.

She stopped, turned to me in confusion. "What *about* your face?"

"Is it long and wrinkled, like Grandmother's, or

round as a coconut, like Star Boy's? Are my eyes wise like yours or ready to laugh like Father's? Are my teeth as crooked as the trunks of palm trees?"

Mother cocked her head to the side and made lines in her forehead. "I don't think I've ever looked at you that way," she said. "To me you've always been yourself, different from anyone else."

"But I want to *know*," I begged her.

Mother nodded. "I remember that feeling. Try this."

She took my hand and guided it to my neck. "Touch," she told me. "Very softly. No, close your eyes and think with your fingers. Now compare." She placed my other hand on her face, the face I knew better than any other.

I traced the line of her chin. Mine was smaller, pointier. I followed her lips with one thumb, my own with the other. Hers seemed fuller.

"Your mouth is wider," I cried, unhappy with myself.

"That's because I'm smiling, Morning Girl."

And suddenly my mouth was wide, too, and my cheeks were hills on either side.

Next I found the lashes of our eyes, then moved

above them. Even without watching I could see the curved shape of Mother's dark brows. They made her look surprised at everything, surprised and delighted.

"Mine are straight," I said.

"Like your grandfather's."

He had always looked tired. I liked surprised better.

"Now, here." Mother cupped my fingers around the tip of my nose. I could feel the breath rush in and out of my nostrils. I could smell the fruit I had picked with Star Boy.

Finally we moved to the ears, and in the dark they were as delicate and complicated as the inside of a spiral shell, but soft.

"Our ears are the same," I told Mother, and she felt with her own hand, testing and probing every part.

"You're right." She sounded as pleased as I was.

I opened my eyes and memorized her ears. At least *that* part I would now recognize.

"Did this help you?" she asked me. "Do you know Morning Girl any better?"

"Oh yes," I said. "She has a chin like a starfish

and brows like white clouds on the horizon. Her nose works. Her cheeks swell into mountains when she smiles. The only thing right about her is her ears."

Mother covered her mouth, the way she does when she laughs and doesn't want anyone to stare. "That's my Morning Girl," she said. "That's her exactly."

The next day, as I was getting up and Star Boy was about to go to sleep on his mat, I leaned close to him.

"What does my chin look like?" I demanded.

He blinked, frowned, made his eyes small while he decided. "A starfish," he finally said.

I was very worried until I saw he was making a joke.

"I heard Mother telling Father," he confessed when I pinched him. "But I don't know." He rubbed his arm, showed me where I had made it turn red. "To me it looks more like the end of the rock that juts out into the ocean near the north end of the island. The one they call 'The Giant Digging Stick.' "

"You don't have to be curious about *your* face," I whispered. "All you have to do is wait for a jellyfish to float on shore and get stranded when the tide leaves. Sometimes I see one and I think it's you, buried in the sand up to your neck."

When I went outside, Father was sitting on a log, fixing a shark's tooth to use as a hook at the end of his fishing lance.

"Who is this?" he asked the lance. "Who is this with my wife's ears stuck onto the side of her head?"

"You laugh at me, too," I said. "But why is it so strange to want to know what everyone else already knows? Why should my own face be a secret from me?"

"There *is* a way," Father said kindly, and motioned me to stand beside him. He knelt down so that we would be the same size. "Look into my eyes," he told me. "What do you see?"

I leaned forward, stared into the dark brown circles, and it was like diving into the deepest pools. Suddenly I saw two tiny girls looking back. Their faces were clear, their brows straight as canoes, and their chins as narrow and clean as lemons. As I watched, their mouths grew wide. They were pretty.

"Who are they?" I couldn't take my eyes off those strange new faces. "Who are these pretty girls who live inside your head?"

"They are the answer to your question," Father said. "And they are always here when you need to find them."

CHAPTER SIX

STAR BOY

The first thing the wind moved was my blood. It ran faster in my arms and legs, pushing against the skin, warning me. I looked east, where the sky was barely turning pink, and instead of being pale, the clouds were the color of dark boulders scattered on a wet beach.

The rain, when it came, didn't fall in the proper way but rushed to the west, fast as a flock of sparrows chasing a hungry gull from their nests. Soon the fronds of the palms and the grasses in the marshy place behind our house were straining in that same direction. The land tried to flatten itself, to become so smooth that the storm could slide across it quickly without hooking on to anything.

I had been outside studying the sky from our cassava patch, had watched the stars drown one by one, and had felt the pull of the storm's tow myself. Our house, just across the short grass from where I lay, leaned and groaned, begging to go. In a flash of lightning, I saw my father standing in the doorway. His hair was flying in all directions at once. Even his eyes seemed to stretch, and there was a worry on his face I had only seen there once before—the time when the bad visitors, their bodies painted white for death, were spotted in three big rafts to the south of the nearest island.

My father called to my mother, and she appeared beside him, holding to his waist with both arms. Next to her, Morning Girl was excited.

"Star Boy," my mother shouted over the wind. She turned her head from side to side, shielding her eyes from the rain with her hand, searching for where I might have gone.

"I'm here," I cried, but my words fled west, too, and never reached her, so I got up and started to cross the clearing to our house. Then I was being pushed, shoved, a giant fist at my back and beneath my knees, and all I could hear was the wail of a hill of noise, the whipping leaves. Sand stung my face, but by squinting I could see Morning Girl pointing in my direction. My father got down on his hands and knees and crawled toward where I was headed, dragging himself forward by reaching first for a stump, then for a rock. Suddenly I was back on the ground, trying to grab on to something myself, something that didn't want to go, but no sooner would my fingers close around a plant than it would break off at the stem, no sooner would my heels find a root than I would be skidded forward, skipping like a flat rock thrown on a pond. The rain was before me and behind me and all around me, a thick crashing wave, and all I knew was water and movement that slammed and hissed and screamed my name.

But no, it was my father's voice, changed by his worry, made louder than I had ever heard it. I couldn't catch all the words, just some, like "find" and "come" and "help," and then a strange calmness poured over my thoughts, and I was watching what was happening to me as if it were happening to someone else. I saw my wet arms, my twisting legs. I saw the roof of our house, the yellow fronds soaked a dark tan, become a winged turtle and swim away from the poles. I saw trees, big and small, crash into one another.

Yet I wasn't afraid. I kept seeing Morning Girl's face, and I felt the same as she had looked: interested, curious, amazed that such weather as this could be. I watched the way you watch when you know you want to remember: Slowly, even though everything was going fast. Carefully, even though everything was confusing. In some part of me I thought that if I noticed each piece of what I saw, I could someday put it all together into a story.

Far away from where I watched, my back was scratched, my hip was bounced on a stone, my chest was squeezed so tightly that it was hard to breathe. Far away from where I listened to the howl of the wind mixed with the shrieks of the birds, I knew I was heading toward an area of the island where no grasses grew, where the coral was sharp and dangerous. Far away from where I loved this storm, I realized it could hurt me. Yet there was no time to be scared and too much to see to close my eyes. I didn't want it to stop.

To my right was a very large tree, a special tree with fingers that dug into the earth. Usually the higher branches were filled with red parrots. It was a place people sat under during important times. The trunk was so broad, the bark so old and carved, that you could find in its designs the faces of all the people who have ever died, if you needed to talk to them once more. We went there to look for the new sister when she didn't come home, and there she was, not far from my grandfather.

Even in the dim gray light, even with the thunder in my ears, even when I lost the sense to know up from down, I could see that I was coming closer and closer to that tree. Then it rose tall before me, and—clear as I knew that Mother was still calling my name, true as I knew that Father was still making his way to the place I had been, sure as I knew that Morning Girl would want to hear all that had happened to me in the storm and be jealous that it had happened to me and not to her—I knew it was the one tree that would surely remain tomorrow in the same spot it had been today.

I couldn't exactly move my body where I wanted

it to go, and I couldn't exactly stop it either, but by throwing my shoulders to one side I managed to shift my course a little bit. So I did it again. And again. And the fourth time, my hand hit against one of the large tree's fingers, I grasped it and held on. A short time later the wind retreated, as if it were sucking in a large breath in order to blow harder, and I took the chance to pull myself closer to the trunk. I was not alone there. Shells and flowers, even a bird and a blue snake, were pressed into the deepest folds of the wood. By making myself very soft, by letting my back find its own way, I fit into a kind of shallow basket that I would have never noticed with my eyes. As long as I kept my balance, leaning toward the opposite direction of where the wind wanted me, I became part of the tree, another face looking out into the world, watching. With my ears so hard against the bark, I could almost hear the others arguing and joking, chanting and singing to themselves in their own language.

The wind was angry that I had discovered how to stop myself. It slapped my cheeks and banged my head and pulled at my elbows. And just as suddenly as it had come, my calmness was gone, yanked away from me.

"Mother," I yelled. "Father. I'm here."

At first there was no answer, nothing beyond the roar, but then . . .

"It's all right, Star Boy," came a gnarled voice, coiled as the twist of knotted wood. "Stay with us, and you will be safe."

It was my grandfather, high above me.

"It's you, isn't it?" I whispered, and he laughed the way I remembered, when he used to hold me against his warm skin and tell me stories about the sort of man I would grow up to be.

"I'll visit with you as long as this storm lasts," he said. "You must sit very still, and you must never tell anyone that I was here or what I say. It will be a secret between us."

"At least one person," I begged him.

"You always argue, Star Boy," he sighed. "All right. Only Morning Girl, but she won't believe you."

Then we talked and talked and talked.

Later, when the rain once again began to seek the ground, when the palm fronds still attached to trees could once again return to their usual shapes, when I caught sight of my mother running toward me through the tangle of broken branches and heard my father promising her that they would find me soon, I thanked my grandfather and told him good-bye.

CHAPTER SEVEN

MORNING GIRL

No one had died. The storm had damaged nothing that could not be built again. Who needed a roof when the sun shone so friendly or when the stars glowed overhead, watching our sleep? The wind had cleared a new path across the island, wide and open, and all along it, the old was suddenly new, made clean, set out in a different way.

Father, Mother, and I followed the wind's trail to find Star Boy tucked in the arms of the tree where the new sister stayed with Grandfather. When we told Grandmother what had happened, how my brother had been caught and protected, her smile took over her whole face, squeezing shut her small, dark eyes and pushing her chin into her chest when she bowed her head. She told us that Grandfather had once saved Father, too, long ago, from a shark—which was how he got his old man's name, Fast Arms.

People from other families couldn't remain at their homes. "Our houses didn't stay put," they joked when they passed us. "Why should we?"

How easy it was, that first long day, to gather what we needed. The palms were already spread on the ground, perfect for thatch. Coconuts lay where they had fallen, and even, in some unexpected places—large puddles or places where the ponds had spilled over their banks—silver fish carried from the sea could amazingly be found.

The high tides had left the beach flat and smooth, and beyond, the water was tipped with gold where the sun patted the rippling waves.

Of course, there was much work to be done . . . but not on the first day, Father decided, and not on the second, either. Instead, he said this was a chance to be happy together, to dance and make music on hollow logs, to watch ball games, to sing good-bye to the wind, and to share the food that had been presented to us as its apology. It was the time for each person to tell a story, to act it out while the rest of us held our heads in fear or covered our mouths when the laughter grew too strong to contain.

Mother found dry sticks and poured fire from her pot, then roasted some sweet potatoes in a pit she dug in the ground. Star Boy and I searched among the trees, looking under branches and drooping leaves to find fruit that had not burst. I tried not to count or notice that I found three more than he did. After all, my arms were longer, and, anyway, I knew his story would be better than mine.

A large crowd of grandparents, adults, children, and babies had already assembled near The Digging Stick, the place where the land rocks curve into the ocean. I was shy at first because of seeing so many people at once—that almost never happened except when there was a marriage or when someone died. Another thing was different, too, though for a while I couldn't place what it was. Then I knew! The wind had swept away most of the tiny bugs, the ones that were all mouth, the ones that ate and ate and were never full. Usually, when the air was still, people had to burn smudge fires or rub ashes and soot on their bodies to discourage the appetites of those bugs. At such times, we turned into a gray people, except for our hair and lips and eyes. But today we were bright as wet shells, each person painted and decorated differently. Some wore flattened gold leaves in their earlobes, some placed hibiscus blooms in their hair or hung long necklaces of shells around their necks.

Wherever I looked there was food, food, food— all the secret recipes from each family there to taste, more food than I had ever seen.

Star Boy, probably because he was so sure his adventure would be admired, was not timid. He raced ahead of us with his hands open and took some wonderful thing to eat from each mat he passed.

I didn't think much of this—I was used to my

brother being a child, and he was simply behaving the way a child behaves, no worse than that. I remembered when I could run free, not worrying that I might appear foolish, and there was a part of me that wished I could join Star Boy now: do whatever I wanted with no aunt's or uncle's eyes to correct me or to embarrass Mother by staring at me too hard. I had received those looks only once, and that had been too much, more than enough to remind me that though I had not yet become a woman, I was no longer a child.

And then, as I watched, I realized that Star Boy was not a child anymore, either, that he had become too old for such play in public, and I saw all around him those terrible looks, pointed at him.

Now he'll learn, I thought, with more rightness than kindness.

But Star Boy didn't notice. His eyes were full of the surprise of not blowing away, too proud, too excited, too—

A big boy, Never Cry, spoke the word I was thinking:

"Hungry!" Never Cry called to my brother. "You're well named."

A few people laughed, and didn't even cover

their mouths. Father touched Mother's arm just above her elbow. Her lips pressed together, and I knew how she felt: how could Star Boy be wrong on so fine a day?

"I'm not Hungry anymore," my brother told Never Cry, loud enough for all to hear. He was so pleased with himself, that he hadn't understood. "I'm Star Boy now, because—"

My uncle, Sharp Tooth, interrupted. "The wind still must be flowing," he said to Father. "It mixes words and meanings. I thought I heard your little Hungry say he had a grown boy's name, but look, he's the same as ever, the same as he has always been."

My brother stopped where he was. His hands were filled with food he couldn't drop and waste. There was fresh honey smeared on his chin. He closed his eyes, then opened them. He looked at me.

I don't know how long we stood that way, but it was as if just the two of us were there. I was aware of the sounds of babies, of waves, of the birds as they flapped their wings above the food, but I heard them through deep water. Star Boy and I reached across the space between us, we made a fishing line with our eyes and each pulled the other to the center.

"Food!" I sang, loud as my voice would reach. "Food! I'm so hungry I can't wait any longer to eat!"

I ran through the crowd, following the path my brother had broken, sampling and reaching like the youngest child, filling my mouth until I couldn't talk, until I reached Star Boy.

It was so quiet I could hear my mouth chewing.

"Let us *eat*!" called Father, behind me. "This family is hungry. We forgot food while we searched for our son, Star Boy, who watches over us during the night. Now our stomachs rule our brains."

I turned and glanced up quickly, watched as Father took a fruit in each hand and lifted them to his face. The juice ran down his chest as he took bite after bite.

"Perhaps *you* are not hungry, little Sharp Tooth," my mother said to her brother. "Perhaps you slept when the wind passed over, or perhaps you are not hungry because you are already too heavy for even a hurricane to lift. But me, *I* am hungry."

"Me, too," growled the voice of Grandmother, off to the side of where I stood staring at the ground before my feet.

"And me," said our neighbor I Swam Too Far, who had helped us search for Star Boy.

The tide had changed, and people began to look at my uncle instead of at my brother and me. For a moment, his face grew full of the anger that comes from being wrong, but then, swift as yesterday's rain had departed, he set it free.

"Star Boy," Sharp Tooth called. "Bring me some sweet lemon. Find me a coconut to drink. Let me be the first to know your story so that I can introduce my nephew by his proper name when you tell everyone else what happened."

Names are strange and special gifts. There are names you give to yourself and names you show to the world, names that stay for a short while and names that remain with you forever, names that come from things you do and names that you receive as presents from other people. No one would forget that my brother had once been Hungry, but today they would listen for who he had become. And Star Boy, too, would remember that he was now older, that he could no longer behave as a child. If your name is true, it is who you are.

I swallowed the last of the food in my mouth and lifted my eyes. Star Boy had not moved.

"It's all right," I whispered to him. "Go."

And he did, finally, but not before he spoke so that only I could hear, not before he had called me the name he would always afterward use when we were alone together, not before he had said, so softly, "The One Who Stands Beside."

CHAPTER   EIGHT

CHAPTER   EIGHT

STAR BOY

First, I got mad at my best friend, Red Feathers. He came to my house in the afternoon, the way he always does, and we went off to explore that place on the island where the wind had swept the parts of many houses. I wanted to look for our roof, and maybe for my collection of pure white conch shells, each one perfect, with no holes and no chips missing. They were the only things that I minded losing, and I thought it was possible that the wind had only hidden them from me, played a game I could still win. Red Feathers was good at finding things, which was one of the reasons he was my best friend. And he was glad to be away from his parents, who had been shouting at each other more than usual since the storm.

But halfway into the mess of twisted branches and spiky fronds, Red Feathers stopped and put one hand to his chin, an old man about to be wise.

"I am worried, Star Boy," he said slowly. "Maybe we shouldn't go so far from home."

"Why not?" I wondered if he feared that the wind would come back, bored and looking for company, and without thinking I crouched to the ground.

"Well," Red Feathers went on, his eyes sly. "What if you become hungry again, the way you were yesterday? What if you start to gnaw on bark like a mouse?"

I didn't answer him, just stood up, pushed my way out of the tangle, then walked back down the path and closed my ears.

"Don't be that way, Star Boy," Red Feathers called after me. "It was a joke. I'm only repeating what I heard my brother say to his wife when I told them where I was going today."

I looked very hard at a large tree far in front of me. I filled my eyes with its shape—paid attention to nothing else—and by the time I reached the base of its trunk, Red Feathers had given up, and his words no longer slapped at me.

The next one who made me mad was my father. We sat on the ground together, watching the fire and waiting for a fish wrapped in leaves to steam. I had not eaten since the feast, and not much then, after the first few bites, so the smell of the food was wonderful—rich and thick and curling to the sky. I closed my eyes, and my tongue imagined the taste it would soon welcome. It was so real to me that I must have opened my mouth, just a little.

"It's good to like food," my father said in the voice he used when he was being a father, and woke me back to where I was. "But your enjoyment won't disappear if you hide the loudness of its call."

I blinked, and saw he was smiling. *Smiling!*

"I'm going to the beach," I told him. "Maybe I'll swim to the little island where only birds live."

My father started to speak. For a moment he looked as though he would apologize, ask me to stay and eat the evening meal, but then he stopped himself, sighed, and nodded.

"You're not a child," he said. "You may do as you wish."

And so I had no choice. I left.

Then, still later, beneath a blank sky where clouds had washed away my familiar stars, I got the maddest of all.

"Don't sulk," Morning Girl's voice spoke out of the darkness. "Are you pretending to be a rock again?"

"I'm not," I said, quickly changing my mind. Being a rock was used up.

"Everyone's worried that you're hungry. I told them you wouldn't starve if you missed one night, but Father sent me to bring you back. So come on. I'm tired. I want to go to sleep so that I can wake up early."

"I'm waiting for the stars," I told her.

"You're being a baby. Just because some people laughed at you—"

I put my hands over my ears. Let her talk, I thought. Let her say anything at all. I won't hear.

But Morning Girl's words were a splashing stream that found its way between my fingers, no matter how tightly I pressed them together.

"Grow up," she shouted.

The night hid my anger. It hid my shame. In its blackness, I was the blackest part. If I closed my mind into the deepest chamber of a shell, she would have to go away.

And, finally, she did.

"Stay here, then," she said. "I don't understand you."

I heard her footsteps return toward the fire, and I was alone. Except not really alone: I was still with myself. Now it was my own thoughts that argued inside my head, my own voice that imitated the laughter, that drew me a picture of myself, my hands full of food, standing in the midst of all the people on the island. No one would ever forget my mistake or think of me except as a little child, even if I became an old, old man. I wished again for the island with only birds. I wished the wind had carried me there, carried me anywhere, anywhere but where I was.

After a while, I remembered the last time I had been outside alone at night, when the storm had chased me. The breeze off the sea was chilly on my skin, and in all directions I thought I heard the scurry of small feet, the click of claws, the whisper of animals making plans with each other. There are stories that small children believe, stories about strange happenings, stories that tonight I tried very hard not to tell myself.

When it's light, it's usually possible to measure how far the day has come, how long it has yet to last, by the position of the sun in the sky or by the brightness of the air, but this night there were no markers, at least none that I had learned to understand, to know the distance from beginning to ending. It was like swimming underwater, holding your breath, and having no idea how deep you'd gone. Some people never find their way back from such dives, and now, as the great island above me remained unchanged, I wondered if I had lost the day forever. I touched my face with my fingers, as Morning Girl had told me she had done with my mother. I felt my eyelids close, open, close, open, but either way, I saw the same thing: nothing at all.

I thought of calling Grandfather, of asking him if he wanted to talk some more, but that would be rude. I had disturbed his sleep so recently, and anyway, I remembered how he liked to tease. I knew he would agree that I had behaved foolishly. I thought of going home, of the fish that I was positive had been saved for me, but the one thing I wouldn't do was make Morning Girl right.

When I had nothing else to think of, I simply let the air wash over me. I became the darkness. I listened to my breath as it ran in and out of my mouth like tides on the beach. I put my hands flat on the sand and felt the smoothness against my palms. I sniffed the air, got to know this great, wide house, because I didn't know how long I would have to live in it. And, without my ever noticing the change, I stopped being mad. I became myself.

I must have slept, because I woke up, and three things were different. The biting bugs had returned, the morning star had appeared in the eastern sky, and my mother had come to sit beside me. She was quiet, waiting, her body a dim shape settled so naturally into itself that until she spoke I couldn't be sure that she was not just my wish.

"Tell me what you've learned," she asked, her words low and like a dream.

"At night," I answered in that same whispering tone, "at night you must be your own friend."

My mother took a short breath, and I knew she understood me.

MORNING GIRL

There was still no top on our house, and, especially at night, it was as though we were fish circling in a secret pool whose banks were so steep that the only things we knew about were water and the flat roof of sky.

It had been a long night of waiting: first, for Star Boy. Mother, Father, and I usually didn't talk much when we ate our meal together, but my brother always had something to say. Without him, the silence was very loud. Once, when a bird cried out, and later, when the breeze knocked at the wall, the three of us turned our faces toward the doorway, ready to not notice that Star Boy had finally given up his stupid game. Then, when he didn't appear, we pretended that we had moved for other reasons: Father lit a smudge fire to keep away the insects; Mother shifted to her knees and checked that there was water in her drinking bowl; I scratched my head.

After the sky disappeared, I thanked Mother and Father for my food and went outside, as I always did before sleep. This time, however, I did not walk into the bushes. Instead, I followed the voice of the waves to the beach, where, of course, Star Boy was waiting to be found. I told him that we were worried about him, but he was stubborn and refused to listen. I thought I might remind him of the stories told to small children about the giant starfish who creeps ashore at night, but since I had to go back on the path alone, I decided not to bring up such tales.

At home, the circle of embers burned red in the

center of the room. Mother and Father quickly looked behind me when I appeared at the door, and I saw the disappointment in their faces.

"Well, I found him," I announced.

"Is he with Red Feathers?" Father asked, his frown anxious to be sent away.

Before I could say no, Mother interrupted. "You know Red Feathers is staying at his uncle's," she said in a voice that meant more than the words. I watched Father remember the news that I Swam Too Far had shared, along with some of his catch, when he visited earlier this evening. Nobody had to talk about what everyone already knew: that Red Feather's mother and father were arguing with each other again.

"Did Star Boy tell you how late he would be?" Father wanted to know. "Did you say we had saved his food for him?"

"Probably his stomach is still full from yesterday." I spoke before I could stop myself, and Father bit his lip. He was about to reply when Mother picked up her bowl and poured water around the edges of the coals.

"Sleep now," she said through the smoke. Her

voice was not exactly angry at me, but it was not proud of me, either.

More waiting, more listening, more wondering as we each lay awake, our thoughts woven together. Star Boy filled the house by not being inside it, just as, I thought, he had hoped to do.

After a long time of quiet, Mother moved softly past me, slipped outside. Afterward, Father turned where he lay, and now we began to wait for her, too.

There was no hope of sleep. I would almost doze off when I'd hear Father stretch, swing slowly to his feet, and make his way to the doorway. I imagined him looking into the night, listening for the beat of Mother's and Star Boy's feet on the path, straining for the carry of their voices on the breeze. He'd remain that way so long that my mind would finally begin to drift. My eyelids would get heavier, the mat beneath me would become more comfortable, the dance of my ideas would sway, and then . . . Father would clear his throat or mumble to himself or bump my leg as he returned to sit in his hammock, and I would be completely alert.

At last, just when the sky was turning gray with morning, usually my favorite time, I sank into a heavy sleep. The next moment I heard real footsteps, and through the slit of my eyes I watched Mother enter. She carried Star Boy like a baby in her arms, sang a thin song into his ear, and gently settled him down onto his sleeping mat. He was so tired he hardly moved. Father leaned over and stretched out one arm to touch my brother's head, then Mother's hand.

"The bugs have bitten you," he whispered.

"Not badly," she said. Still, she let him draw her into his hammock, and I heard them talking softly together, heard Father laugh at something Mother told him. It would be a late morning for everyone, except for me.

I stepped over my mat very carefully and left the house. I set my feet into the hard-packed places, turned sideways to avoid the leaves of plants, ducked beneath low branches. From my quick dream I chose the idea of water, maybe because I was thirsty, maybe because the day was already hot and the thought of waves on my skin made me feel better, maybe because the sea promised me a story.

Smoke was not yet rising from cook fires, so I knew it was early. No wonder the sea called. It must be lonely, a feeling I could understand: today, I was in no one's good thoughts. Star Boy was unhappy with me, and now Mother and Father were, too, for their own reasons. They would be distant toward me until I helped them to forget my unsisterly words.

I wished there were someone I could complain to, someone who would easily forgive me either for being too nice, as I was to Star Boy at the feast, or too harsh, as I was last night. I missed the new sister who had never come home. I was sure I would never have argued with her. It seemed to me wrong that she had received no name. Grandmother said that we hadn't known her well enough . . . and yet I *did* know her. She was in my thoughts often, as she was this morning. Then I had an idea so surprising that I stopped walking: *I* could give the new sister a name, just between her and me. I closed my eyes, held my breath, and found exactly the right one: She Listens. Now she was real.

I looked at the place where I was, to remember it. The island was all green and brown, the flowers red and yellow, the sky a deep and brilliant blue. At my feet, the tip of something white stuck from the sand. I stooped, dug with my fingers, and pried out a small, empty conch, washed so gently by the sea that not a single chip was missing—just the way Star Boy insisted for the shells he liked to keep. My gift would be the start of his new collection, replacing what the storm had borrowed. Things would be the way they had been, only better. I put the conch into a bowl of dried seaweed, where I could find it later, and ran into the water.

Dawn made a glare on the ocean, so I splashed through the shallow surf and dived without looking. I felt the hair lift from around my head, felt a school of tiny fish glide against my leg as I swam underwater. Then, far in the distance, I heard an unfamiliar and frightening sound. It was like the panting of some giant animal, a steady, slow rhythm, dangerous and hungry. And it was coming closer.

I forgot I was still beneath the surface until I needed air. But when I broke into the sunlight, the water sparkling all around me, the noise turned out to be nothing! Only a canoe! The breathing was the dip of many paddles! It was only *people* coming to visit, and since I could see they hadn't painted themselves to appear fierce, they must be friendly or lost.

I swam closer to get a better look and had to stop myself from laughing. The strangers had wrapped every part of their bodies with colorful leaves and cotton. Some had decorated their faces with fur and wore shiny rocks on their heads. Compared to us, they were very round. Their canoe was short and square, and, in spite of all their dipping and pulling, it moved so slowly. What a backward, distant island they must have come from. But really, to laugh at guests, no matter how odd, would be impolite, especially since I was the first to meet them. If I was foolish, they would think they had arrived at a foolish place.

"I won't make a mistake," I told She Listens. "I won't be too good, and I won't say too much because I might choose the wrong words."

I kicked toward the canoe and called out the simplest thing.

"Hello!"

One of the people heard me, and he was so startled that he stood up, made his eyes small, as fearful as I had been a moment earlier. Then he spotted me, and I waved like I've seen adults do when visitors arrive, my fingers spread to show that my hand was empty.

The man stared at me as though he'd never seen a girl before, then shouted something to his relatives. They all stopped paddling and looked in my direction.

"Hello," I tried again. "Welcome to home. My name is Morning Girl. My mother is She Wins the Race. My father is Speaks to Birds. My brother is Star Boy. We will feed you and introduce you to everyone."

All the fat people in the canoe began pointing at me and talking at once. In their excitement they almost turned themselves over, and I allowed my body to sink beneath the waves for a moment in order to hide my smile. One must always treat guests with respect, I reminded She Listens, even when they are as brainless as gulls.

When I came up they were still watching, the way babies do: wide eyed and with their mouths uncovered. They had much to learn about how to behave.

"Bring your canoe to the beach," I shouted, saying each word slowly so that they might understand and calm themselves. "I will go to the village and bring back Mother and Father for you to talk to."

Finally one of them spoke to me, but I couldn't understand anything he said. Maybe he was talking Carib or some other impossible language. But I was sure that we would find ways to get along together. It never took that much time, and acting out your thoughts with your hands could be funny. You had to guess at everything and you made mistakes, but by midday I was certain we would all be seated in a circle, eating steamed fish and giving each other presents. It would be a special day, a memorable day, a day full and new.

I was close enough to shore now for my feet to touch bottom, and quickly I made my way to dry land. The air was warm against my shoulders, and there was a slight breeze that disturbed the palm fronds strewn on the ground. I squeezed my hair, ran my hands over my arms and legs to push off the water, and then stamped on the sand.

"Leave your canoe right here," I suggested in my most pleasant voice. "It will not wash away, because the tide is going out. I'll be back soon with the right people."

The strangers were drifting in the surf, arguing among themselves, not even paying attention to me any longer. They seemed very worried, very confused, very unsure what to do next. It was clear that they hadn't traveled much before.

I hurried up the path to our house, but not before She Listens reminded me to take the white conch shell from the seaweed where I had left it. As I dodged through the trees, I hoped I hadn't done anything to make the visitors leave before I got back, before we learned their names. If they were gone, Star Boy would claim that they were just a story, just my last dream before daylight. But I didn't think that was true. I knew they were real.